PLANET HELL

To Readers, Every One of You, Everywhere!

First published 2012 by A & C Black,
an imprint of Bloomsbury Publishing Plc
50 Bedford Square, London WC1B 3DP

www.acblack.com
www.bloomsbury.com

ISBN 978-1-4081-5477-9

A CIP catalogue for this book is available from the British Library.

Printed by CPI Group (UK), Croydon, CR0 4YY

1 3 5 7 9 10 8 6 4 2

recommended by

www.catchup.org

Catch Up is a not-for-profit charity
which aims to address the problem of
underachievement that has its roots in
literacy and numeracy difficulties.

PLANET HELL

Joan Lennon

A & C Black • London

Contents

Chapter 1

Dead End

It was dark in the tunnel. Dead dark. But Sam didn't need to see. He knew every tunnel and cave in the Mine.

It was too bad the Gang chasing him did too.

Sam could hear the Gang getting closer. He covered his breathing mask with his hands and tried not to make a sound.

All the miners wore masks to keep the deadly Mine dust out of their lungs.

"Nice work, kid," one of the Gang shouted. "You've run into a dead end. There's no way out."

"You've been making trouble – again," shouted another voice. "You've been asking too many questions."

"We don't like people who ask questions," called another man. "We are going to teach you a lesson. You've had your last chance."

Somebody laughed. Cold sweat ran down Sam's back.

Sam tried to think. He knew there must be a way into the air shaft from this tunnel. There should be a small opening covered by a metal grill. But where was it?

At last his fingers found the metal grill. The opening was tiny, but the air shaft on the other side would be big enough to crawl through.

Suddenly, Sam felt something move under his hand. It was hard and smooth, like a bottle.

He didn't stop to think. He grabbed the bottle, swung his arm and hit the man in the face.

Sam heard the man's breathing mask crack. He heard the man shout and swear. But he didn't wait to see what happened next.

Sam turned and fled into the darkness.

Chapter 2

Too Many Questions

The Miners had lived underground on
Planet Hell for hundreds of years. They
drilled Ore out of the rock. Then they turned
the Ore into power.

The power was sent up to the Surface of Hell, and beamed back to Planet Earth.

People always said that if you worked very hard, the Mining Company would send you home to Earth, as a reward.

Sam's dad had been sick with lung rot from the Mine dust. Sam kept saying, "Please, send him back to Earth. He's worked hard in the Mine all his life. He deserves to go back home to Earth!"

But nobody listened. And then, it was too late. His dad was dead. The lung rot killed him.

That was why Sam began to ask questions. If his dad didn't deserve to go home, who did?

He asked everyone, saying, "Do you know anybody who got sent back to Earth? Do you? Anybody?"

Everybody knew stories about someone who had been sent back to Earth. But nobody knew anybody real, with a real name, and a real life. All they had were stories.

Soon the Gang found out about Sam's questions. And they were very, very angry.

Sam's mum had died when he was a baby, so his dad had brought him up.

When Sam was little, his dad told him stories about Planet Earth.

"Earth is all blue and green, and you can live on the Surface there," he said. "The sun shines in the sky and the air is fresh and clean. That's where our people come from."

"Will I get to go there one day?" Sam asked.

"One day, if you work very hard," said Sam's dad.

But it hadn't turned out like that.

Now Sam was all alone, and the Gang was
after him.

"I wish you were here, Dad," Sam
whispered in the darkness. "I wish you were
here."

Chapter 3

Message in a Bottle

Sam was still hiding in the air shafts.
He was panting hard. He could hear a huge
digging machine bashing out a new tunnel
nearby. BAM … BAM … BAM …

Sam lit an electric candle and looked down. He still had the bottle in his hand. Suddenly, he saw something inside the bottle…

He took the top off the bottle, turned it upside down and shook it. A piece of paper fell out. It had writing on it in large letters.

Hey! Trolls!
If you're really down there,
come and get me!
I'm not afraid of you!

Sam turned the piece of paper over. On the back in much smaller writing it said:

> *I only wrote that message because they made me. If you are real, please, please don't come up!*

Sam read it three times. It didn't make any sense.

Who can have written it? he wondered.

Sam's dad had taught him how to write all the letters – but not like this. Not with all those loops and curly bits. Sam didn't know anybody in the Mine who could write like that.

It was almost as if somebody from the Surface had written the message. Put it in the bottle. Thrown it down the air shaft.

But that's just stupid – no one can live on the Surface! Sam thought. Of course, there were lots of stories about horrible monsters living up there. They had no eyes and ate rock and drank each other's boiling blood. But the stories were just to scare little kids.

His dad had told him all about what it was really like on the Surface. There was blazing sun and terrible heat. The air was full of poison. The land was all burned up.

"That's why they called this Planet Hell," his dad had said.

Sam shoved the bottle into his pocket. He just wanted to go home. He crept along the air shafts until he came to a secret opening at the back of his cave. It was covered with a metal grill. He reached out to pull it open – and froze.

He heard a sound.

Sam peered into his cave. He'd left an electric candle lit, but it was dying now. The room was almost dark. Then Sam saw a shape move in the shadows.

The Gang had got there before him.

Chapter 4

Going Up

Sam tried to stop shaking.

What could he do? The Gang knew every part of the Mine. There was nowhere to hide.

He looked at the bottle with the message inside.

Everyone says that nobody can live on the Surface, he thought. *But what if everyone is wrong? I could go and find out. After all, what have I got to lose?*

There was no way but up.

*   *   *

Sam started to climb through the air shafts.

The air for the Mines came from the Surface. There were filters to take the poison out of it. And there were huge fans with sharp spinning blades to blow the fresh air into the tunnels.

28

The blades made cutting sounds as they slid past each other. **Shiiiip. Shiiiip.** Then the blades would stop dead for a moment, and then start spinning the other way, to blow the used air out again.

That will be my moment, thought Sam. *When the blades stop. That's when I'll climb through.*

The air shafts ran for miles. It would be easy to get lost. But Sam's dad had taught him how to see the whole Mine in his mind in 3D. Like a map, only better.

Sometimes the air shafts passed by other Miners' caves. Sam could hear people talking and moving about. It made him feel lonely.

It made him want to turn back.

Then he felt the bottle in his pocket.

Come on, Sam, he told himself. *Keep moving.*

Suddenly he heard it. The sound he had been dreading.

The sound of the fan.

The blades of the fan sliced through the air at a terrible speed. Sam listened hard, waiting for the sound to change.

There! The blades were slowing down. The fast slicing sound was becoming a slower *shiiiiip ... shiiiiip ...*

Now! Without stopping to think, Sam scrambled up the air shaft towards the fan.

Shiiiiippppp ...

And silence. The fan was still.

With shaking hands, Sam reached up and touched the razor sharp metal. He pushed the blades apart and started to pull himself through the narrow gap. He felt his shirt catch and rip. Then he heard the fan's engine starting up again, getting ready to turn the fan in the other direction.

He climbed as fast as he could and dragged his foot through the gap just as the blades started to spin again.

Sam carried on, his heart beating fast as the deadly blades sliced through the air below him.

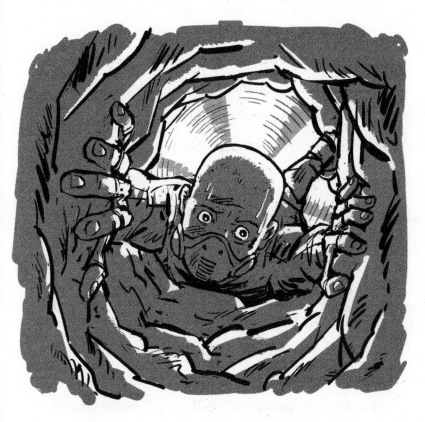

One slip, he thought, *and I'll be cut into bits. No one will ever know what happened to me. No one will know, and no one will care.*

Sam gritted his teeth, and went on climbing.

Chapter 5

Snip, Snap!

On the Surface of Hell, a girl called Anna woke up crying.

Her robot came into her bedroom, sat on the side of her bed and stroked Anna's long hair.

Everyone on Hell was cared for by robots.

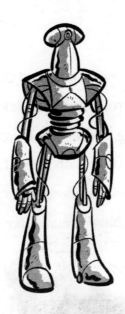

The children had to go to school, but the
adults could do anything they wanted. All the
hard work was done by the robots. The robots
took care of everything.

"Oh dear – what is the matter?" asked the
robot.

"Nothing," said Anna, rubbing the tears
from her face. But it was a lie.

Anna had been having bad dreams again. Dreams about trolls living under the ground who were going to drag her away.

Anna was angry with herself. *I'm too old to be having dreams about trolls*, she thought. *Only little kids have dreams like that!*

Her robot looked at her. "Are you unhappy? What can I do to help?"

"It's nothing," lied Anna. "I'm fine."

But really, she was very unhappy indeed.

Life on the Surface of Planet Hell was good. Robots did everything to keep the humans safe and happy. In school, the robot teachers said, "This planet is a miracle. The Final War on Earth meant that no creatures could live there any more. The humans had to find another home. When they landed here, they called it Hell because it looked like a world of fire and nothing else. But there *was* something else. There was power. Endless, free power."

When Anna was little, she asked, "Where does the power come from?"

"From under the ground," said the robot teachers. "When they first came to the planet, the humans took apart the space ship they'd come in and built robots out of its parts. And with the help of the robots, they built the force fields."

Everybody knew how important the force fields were.

"The force fields keep out the harmful rays of the sun so that we can live on a clean, safe planet," said the robot teachers. "Without the force fields, the last of the humans would die out. We need the power from under the ground to keep the force fields going."

The power came up a shaft from deep
inside Planet Hell. There were other shafts
too, hidden in caves in the hills.

The air coming up from these holes was hot and smelled bad, like rotten eggs. And sometimes, if you listened hard, you could hear things. Clanking and bashing noises, or metal sliding across metal with a slicing sound.

In the playground, the big kids said, "It's the trolls! When a baby troll is born the mummy troll cuts off its leg, *SNIP!* and cuts off its hand, *SNAP!* and then she sews on a metal leg and a scissor hand. That's their metal legs you hear, clanking, and their scissor hands, slicing. The trolls come up out of the ground in the middle of the night when you're asleep. They sneak into your bedroom and *SNIP!* they cut off your leg. Then *SNAP!* they cut off your hand!"

All the little kids would scream and giggle.

Except for Anna. She just screamed.

Now she was one of the big kids, and she was still scared.

I don't believe in trolls! she told herself again and again. *Don't be such a cry baby!*

But she couldn't stop being scared.

And then things got worse.

Jen, the biggest bully in the school, found out about Anna's fears.

Chapter 6

Cry Baby

Jen gave Anna's arm a hard pinch. "Did you throw the message in the bottle down the hole like I said? Don't you dare lie to me!"

Anna nodded. "Yes! Let go! I did it, just like you said."

The other girls were laughing at how scared Anna was.

"What a cry baby!" they whispered.

"There was a metal grill over the hole but I pushed the bottle through," cried Anna.

"Good," said Jen. "Now the trolls will read what you wrote. And they'll come and snip off your leg and snap off your hand and sew on metal ones. And then they'll drag you under the ground. They won't let you go till you're an old, crazy woman!"

"Oh look, she's crying again," the other girls giggled.

"Bye-bye, cry baby," said Jen and walked away.

"I'm not! I'm not!" Anna sobbed. But she knew they were right. She *was* a cry baby.

She hated herself.

*   *   *

Anna's robot found her lying on her bed.

"Are you unhappy? What is the matter?" asked the robot.

"Nothing's the matter!" cried Anna. "Just leave me alone!"

"If that will make you happy," said her robot.

Anna ran out of the house.

Every time a robot saw her, it stopped working and asked, "Are you unhappy? How can I help you?"

But Anna just ran on.

Anna didn't notice that Jen was following her. She didn't think about where she was going.

She just ran on and on until she realised that she'd come up the path to a cave. The same cave where she'd thrown the message in the bottle down the hole!

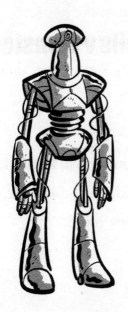

Chapter 7

Trolls v Monsters

Sam was climbing in the dark now. His last electric candle had died. He wasn't sure where he was any more.

Don't panic, Sam, he told himself. *You must be close now.*

His arms and legs shook with tiredness. Hand over hand he climbed, and then suddenly Sam realised – he could *see* his hands!

There was light up above.

This must be it, he thought. *This must be the Surface…*

"OW!"

Sam had banged his head on a metal grill.
He gripped it and pushed hard. For a moment
the grill stuck, and then it fell back and Sam
pulled himself up and over the edge.

He was in a cave, but even in the shadows
the light was so bright it was like a knife in his
eyes. Tears ran down his face, but he forced
his eyes open. He crawled to the opening of
the cave. What he saw made his head spin.

This can't be real! he thought. *Where's the boiling rock? Where's the burned ground? And the poisoned air?*

The Surface of Planet Hell was beautiful.

There were bright colours everywhere –
green fields, buildings painted red and gold
and purple, blue streams and white paths.
Moving about were shiny silver figures, like
human-shaped machines. Sam took off his
breathing mask and sniffed. The air was clean
and pure.

Then he looked up. There was no stone
roof over his head, just empty space that went
higher and higher. It made him feel dizzy and
he looked down quickly with a gulp.

Where are the monsters? he wondered.

And then he heard one – a monster coming up the path towards the cave. It was moving fast and making a lot of noise. It sounded huge and dangerous and angry!

Sam tried to hide but in his panic he couldn't find the opening to the air shaft. Too late! He heard the monster stop and gasp. It had seen him.

Slowly, Sam turned around. He squinted at the monster. It had a huge head and a tall body, like a giant mushroom. It wasn't very big for a monster – about the size of a person – but for a mushroom it was gigantic!

Sam shut his eyes tight and pulled the
bottle out of his pocket. He held it out.

"Is this yours?" he asked.

The monster spoke. "I sent a message in a bottle to the trolls! Please, please don't cut off my hand!"

"What?" said Sam. "Cut off your hand? That's horrible! Why would I want to do that?"

He opened his eyes wide for a second but the light hurt horribly. He cried out with pain.

"Here," said the monster. "Put my hat on."

Sam opened his eyes a little and saw the monster was taking its head off! He nearly choked with fear. Then he looked again. The monster was just taking off a big round hat!

"It will stop the light hurting your eyes," said the monster.

Sam took the hat and put it on. He felt silly, but at least he could see better.

But what he saw didn't make sense.

The monster wasn't a monster at all. It was a girl. Except she wasn't like any girl he'd ever seen before.

She didn't have a shaved head like all the Miners. Instead, she had long hair. She wasn't wearing the dark, heavy Miners' clothes that didn't show the dirt or rip easily. Her clothes were floaty and glittery and changed colour when she moved.

"I can't believe you're here!" said the girl. "Are all trolls like you? You don't seem as scary as in my dreams. All my life I've been terrified of trolls. I've been such a stupid cry baby!"

"Shh! What was that?" cried Sam. He thought he'd heard something outside the cave, but Anna shook her head.

"There's nobody here but me."

They did not see Jen peeping into the cave. They did not hear her run away again.

"I'm Sam," he said. "I don't know why you keep talking about trolls. I don't even know what trolls are! I'm human."

Anna stared. "I'm Anna. And *I'm* human. My people come from another planet. Planet Earth."

"No, that can't be right," said Sam. "That's where the Miners came from. *My* people."

"What miners?" said Anna. "We've been here for a really long time and I never heard anything about miners."

Sam's mouth went dry. "How long?" he asked.

"I'm not sure," said Anna. "We learned all about it in school but, well, I didn't really listen. The War is over. Earth is dead. So who cares?"

"*What* did you say about Earth?" gasped Sam.

Anna looked surprised. "I said Earth is dead. Because of the Final War killing everything. That's why we left. You must know that."

"That can't be true," cried Sam. "Earth can't be dead. It can't be! The Mine is here to make power for Earth. We work for the Mining Company. We're very important. We dig the Ore that makes the power and then we send the power back to Earth. We've been sending power home for hundreds of years…"

Anna looked at him in horror.

"Oh Sam," she whispered. "We didn't know."

Chapter 8

The End of Earth

Sam's heart hurt.

"What didn't you know?" he asked. "I don't understand."

Anna swallowed hard. She tried to remember her school lessons. "There was a Mining Company. The robots told us about that. That was before the Final War. The Mining Company sent out ships to explore. They were looking for new power. That was when they thought the Earth could be saved. But it couldn't. It was too late. Everyone had to leave."

"But the ships?" asked Sam. "The ones looking for new power?"

"Nobody ever heard from them again," said Anna. "I think the Mining Company ended at the same time Earth did. Everything was a mess at the end."

Sam looked at her. He couldn't believe what he was hearing.

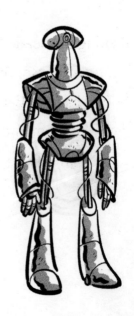

Anna said, "My people were the last to get away from Earth. And then they travelled for such a long time before they found Hell. They only stopped here because the ship was damaged. They thought they were going to die here. Then they found the power supply coming from the ground. They took the ship apart and built the robots out of it, to take care of us."

Sam was shaking his head. "No. No! You're not making any sense. We've been here, sending power back to Earth for more years than anybody can remember. Earth needs us. We keep it going!"

"The power didn't get to Earth, Sam. We found it, when we got here. So we used it. We thought it was free."

"Free? FREE?" shouted Sam.

He had picked up the bottle again and was holding it like a weapon.

Anna stepped back. He was scaring her.

"There it is! There's the troll! Kill it!" cried a voice.

It was Jen, standing at the opening of the cave. And behind her was a silver robot holding a laser gun.

"You have been crying," the robot said to Anna. "Are you unhappy?"

"Yes. I mean, no!" said Anna and at the same moment Sam shouted, "I'm not a troll! I'm a human!"

The robot was confused. "You say you are a human? But she says you are a troll? You are making these humans unhappy? I must speak to the other robots. Trolls do not exist. Trolls are just stories, told by the humans to make themselves happy. Humans like scary stories."

"I'm not a story," yelled Sam. "And I'm not a troll. I'm me. A human. A Miner."

"What are you waiting for?" Jen shouted at the robot. "Kill it! Before it kills us!"

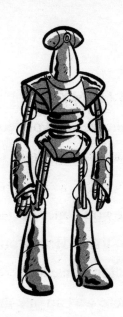

But the robot just stood there. It had frozen up. Robots went like that when they needed to talk with all the other robots.

Jen dragged the gun from its hand and aimed it at Sam. Without thinking, Anna stepped in front of Sam.

"Get out of my way!" hissed Jen. "I'm going to kill it before it kills us!"

But Anna shook her head.

"GET OUT OF MY WAY!" screamed Jen and she shut her eyes and pulled the trigger.

There was a flash of bright light from the gun.

"What have you done?" cried the robot, coming back to life. "Have you killed them?"

But Jen couldn't answer.

Because there was no one there. Sam and Anna had disappeared.

Chapter 9

Going Underground

Down, down. Sam and Anna were sliding
down the air shaft, out of control. Anna didn't
know what was happening.

Sam had grabbed her and jumped back and suddenly the floor disappeared and she was falling through the dark.

But Sam knew what was happening.

We're going to die … we're going to die … we're going to die! The words were screaming in his head, as they crashed down the air shaft, faster and faster, until…

Something caught them.

Someone had put a net across the shaft.

Anna and Sam were bruised, and out of breath, hurting and scared. But they weren't dead.

Yet.

"Looks like we've caught something," a voice called out.

"Gotcha!" said someone else.

Sam groaned. He knew those voices.
Someone lit an electric candle and Sam saw
the Gang staring down at him.

"Did you really think you could get away
from us?" one of them hissed.

"We knew you'd have to come back this
way, once you found out what the Surface was
really like," said another. "No one can live up
there."

The Gang tipped up the net but they had caught more than they expected.

As soon as they saw Anna, the Gang stepped back and stared at her in shock.

"Who is that?"

"This is Anna," said Sam. "She lives on the Surface."

"Don't be stupid," said one of the Gang. "No one can live on the Surface!"

"*She* does," said Sam. "Tell them, Anna."

But Anna was shaking with fear. Sam remembered what she'd said about being afraid of trolls.

"Take off your breathing masks," he said to the Gang. "Let her see that you're humans too."

The men in the Gang looked at each other.
They didn't know what to do. Slowly, they
took off their masks.

Anna gulped hard and then she did a brave thing.

She said, "We need to talk."

* * *

The men in the Gang took Sam and Anna down, deeper under the ground to the main hall at the heart of the Mine.

As they followed the tunnels down, Sam looked over at Anna. She was starting to panic. He remembered how he'd felt on the Surface.

"Are you OK?" he asked.

"We must be going to the centre of the world!" she cried. "All that rock over my head! I feel like it's going to fall on me!"

"It's OK," he said to her quietly. "Miners like my dad built these tunnels. They'll stand forever. Don't be scared."

Anna gave a little smile.

When they got to the main hall a crowd of Miners was waiting for them.

Sam got up on a table so they could all see him.

"I've been to the Surface," said Sam. "I've found out that lots of the things we thought we knew are wrong. There's another world up there, on the Surface. There are humans living up there. Humans like us." He reached out his hand to Anna and she climbed up on the table beside him. "This is Anna."

Everyone gasped. Voices rose out of the crowd.

"She's not from the Mine!"

"Look at her hair! Look at her clothes!"

"No one can live on the Surface. Except monsters!"

There was a sudden silence.

Sam leaned over and whispered to Anna, "Tell them about the Surface."

Anna's heart was pounding, but she made herself speak. She told them about the people on the Surface. She told them about the Final War. The end of Earth. About how the Surface dwellers thought they were going to die when they landed on Hell, and how the power supply they found saved them. She told them about the robots and the force fields. She told them that nobody knew the Miners were there.

With every word the anger in the hall
grew. Sam could feel it.

"Wait till the Mining Company hears
about this!" one of the Miners called out.

"The Mining Company doesn't exist!"
yelled Sam. "Don't you understand? EARTH
IS DEAD!"

The Miners were all shouting at once.

"We'll never get back to Earth?"

"Earth is dead?"

"It's all their fault…"

"What do we do?"

"Let's stop sending power up to the Surface! Let's see how long they last up there when their force fields come down!"

Suddenly a new voice spoke from the back of the hall.

"Do you know what they are saying on the Surface? They are saying, 'We'll block off the air shafts! Let's see how long they last down there with no air!'"

Chapter 10

New Earth

Everyone turned.

"What's THAT?" cried a young Miner. "Is it a monster?"

A strange silver figure was standing there, looking at them all.

"That's Jen's robot!" gasped Anna.

The Miners stared in silence.

"You can stop the power," the robot said. "They can stop the air. You can have another Final War. That is the way things ended on Earth. You and the humans on the Surface are the only humans left in the universe."

Suddenly, the hall began to fill with silver
robots.

"Sam, look! There's my robot!" said
Anna. "And the teacher robots ... and look,
all the robots!"

"We have talked it over," said Anna's robot quietly. "And there is only one way to make all the humans happy. The robots will take over the Mine."

"What?" shouted the Miners.

"You don't know anything about mining!" said Sam.

"Who will look after us?" cried Anna.

"We will learn how to mine," said Anna's robot. "And the Surface dwellers and the Miners will work together to learn how to look after each other. That is the only way to make all the humans happy."

"I don't understand," moaned an old Miner. "All I ever wanted was to go home!"

"Don't you see?" said the robot. "This *is* home."

* * *

It took a long time. Not all the Miners wanted to stop mining. They were scared of the Surface, of the burning sun, and the sky so far away. And not all the Surface dwellers wanted to start farming and cooking and cleaning and teaching and all the other things the robots had been doing for so long.

But slowly, slowly, it happened.

The day finally came when Sam made the long climb up out of the Mine again. This time he didn't have to crawl through darkness or the slicing blades of the fans. This time he wasn't running away. This time he walked up the new stairs knowing that Anna would be at the top.

I wish you were here, Dad, thought Sam. *I wish you were here to see this.*

Sam smiled. He was about to start a
new life. And Planet Hell was about to get
a new name. New Earth.